Edison & Ford
WINTER ESTATES
Homes • Gardens • Laboratory • Museum ™

TABLE OF CONTENTS

(1a)

(1b)

D1451052

(1c)

GUIDE MAP

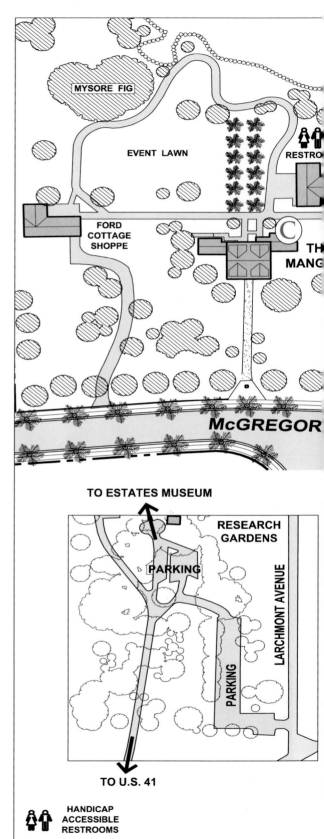

MYSORE FIG

EVENT LAWN

RESTRO

FORD COTTAGE SHOPPE

C

TH MANG

McGREGOR

TO ESTATES MUSEUM

RESEARCH GARDENS

PARKING

LARCHMONT AVENUE

PARKING

TO U.S. 41

HANDICAP ACCESSIBLE RESTROOMS

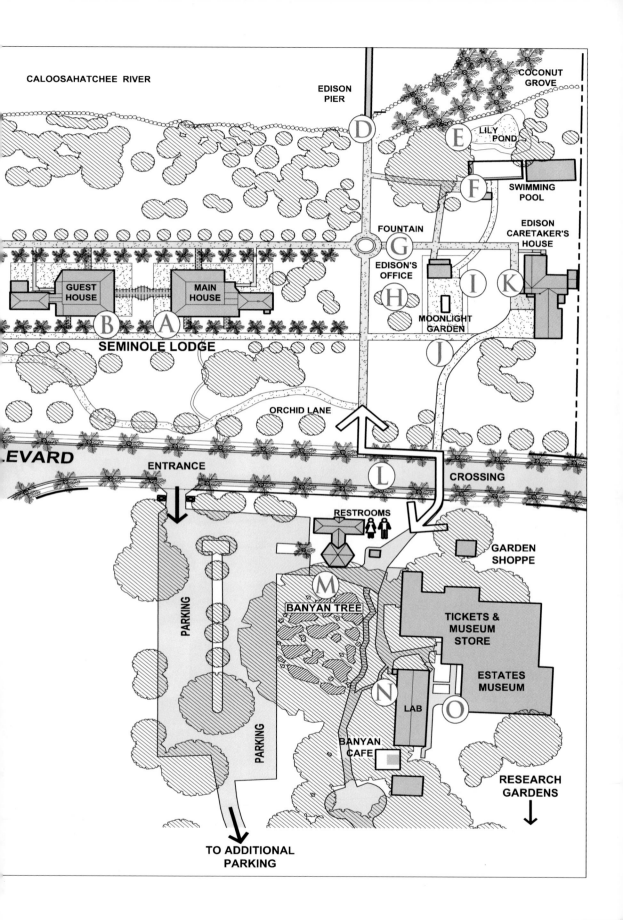

CALOOSAHATCHEE RIVER

EDISON PIER

COCONUT GROVE

LILY POND

D

E

SWIMMING POOL

F

EDISON CARETAKER'S HOUSE

FOUNTAIN

G

EDISON'S OFFICE

I

K

H

MOONLIGHT GARDEN

GUEST HOUSE

MAIN HOUSE

J

B

A

SEMINOLE LODGE

ORCHID LANE

LEVARD

ENTRANCE

L

CROSSING

RESTROOMS

GARDEN SHOPPE

M

BANYAN TREE

TICKETS & MUSEUM STORE

PARKING

ESTATES MUSEUM

N

LAB

O

PARKING

BANYAN CAFE

RESEARCH GARDENS

TO ADDITIONAL PARKING

Thomas Edison first visited Fort Myers, Florida in March of 1885. A successful and famous inventor by this time, Edison was eager to find a warm escape during the winter months from his New Jersey home base. He purchased over 13 acres along the Caloosahatchee River and created an estate that included two homes and Laboratory.

RIGHT: The Family Wing, circa 1901. Architect Alden Frink of Boston helped Edison design the style of his Florida residence. The materials for all of the buildings were pre-made in Maine, shipped down to Fort Myers and built on-site in 1886. (4a)

BELOW: The Family Wing today. Mina Edison deeded the property to the City of Fort Myers to provide the public the opportunity to experience the estate as the Edison family did for many years from 1886 through 1947. (4b)

The Edison Family shared the Estate, named *Seminole Lodge* in honor of a local Indian Tribe, with family and friends. After arriving in Fort Myers from a trip that took many days, guests would stay for weeks or months. Favorite activities included fishing, boating, reading, playing board games, picnics, and walks around the grounds.

RIGHT: Friends pose near a row of Royal Palm Trees that creates one of the many alleé pathways situated on the grounds. (5a)

BELOW: Daughter Madeleine and friends formed a sewing circle on the Verandah in 1912, which remains an ideal spot for visitors to gather. (5b)

BELOW: The Verandah today displays several pieces of the Edison Bar Harbor-style wicker furniture continuing to illustrate the casual, comfortable lifestyle enjoyed at *Seminole Lodge*. (5c)

A Edison's Seminole Lodge
FAMILY WING

LEFT: Edison designed and manufactured "Electrolier" lighting fixtures in the early 1880s to accommodate his newest invention. The Fort Myers Estate has 15 located throughout the two homes. This one provides light to the Family Wing Den. (6a)

BELOW: The Family Home Living Room contains additional casual Bar Harbor-style wicker furniture as placed on the Verandah. Mina Edison provided entertainment by playing the George Steck grand piano. (6b)

BOTTOM RIGHT: The wing addition of the home was originally the kitchen for the Edison Family. In 1910 this area was modeled into a bedroom for Thomas and Mina. Eventually, this became only Mina's bedroom while Thomas retreated to his "doghouse." (6c)

BELOW: The telephone Mina used remains on her writing desk, as does stationery, paperclips and pens. (6d)

EDISON'S SEMINOLE LODGE

LEFT: The "doghouse" bedroom of Thomas Edison is situated on the second floor of the Family Home. His sons, Charles and Theodore, originally used the room that is accessible by an exterior staircase built in 1910. In later years, it provided a private space for Thomas, as well as the opportunity to go to bed in the late hours without disturbing Mina. (7a)

RIGHT: Thomas could sit out on the "doghouse" balcony and enjoy the spectacular view to the river, and perhaps quietly consider his next research project. (7b)

BOTTOM RIGHT: One of two bedrooms located in the main section of the Family Wing. Such furnishings are found in all of the Estate's bedrooms and the sets include a dresser, washstand, quilt rack, small writing desk, and comfortable wicker chairs. (7c)

BELOW: The Edison family purchased many items for the homes from Proctor & Company of New York City. This document is a box list of furnishings for the living and dining rooms shipped to Fort Myers in 1910. (7d)

RIGHT: The Edisons first decided to paint the home gray in 1910, however the roof color has always been red. (8a)

BELOW: (l to r) Carolyn, Mina and her sister Mary relax on the Verandah. (8b)

LEFT: Thomas and Mina Edison at right, along with family and friends, gather under the shade of a large oak tree. (8c)

BELOW: One of Thomas' favorite hobbies was to read. With books stacked on the table, Edison looks through a newspaper. (8d)

BOTTOM LEFT: Charles Edison caught this large tarpon in the Caloosahatchee River at age 14. Charles related later in life that it was the only time he beat his father at something, and it was remembered as a family joke for years. (9a)

BELOW: Thomas and Mina stroll along the Main Gate alleé in 1912. (9b)

Edison's Seminole Lodge
FAMILY WING

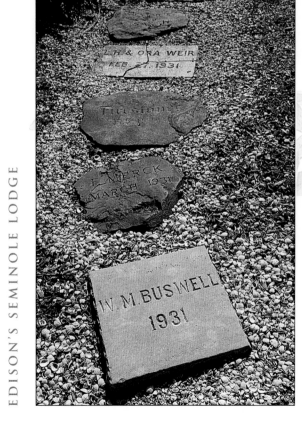

ABOVE: Over 50 stones create The Friendship Walk that winds towards the Family Wing. (10a)

LEFT: The Friendship Walk began in 1928, influenced by a similar walk located at Rollins College in Winter Park, Florida. Dr. Hamilton Holt, President of the College, gave the first stone. Other stones are from friends such as Henry Ford and Harvey Firestone, local dignitaries and employees of *Seminole Lodge*. (10b)

BELOW: Mina Edison wrote correspondence to family and friends routinely. This letter to her mother is written from *Seminole Lodge* on February 15, 1910. Mina tells about a planned morning walk to downtown Fort Myers for "good exercise and do the marketing." (10c)

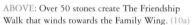

RIGHT: The Edison Guest Wing of *Seminole Lodge*, circa 1886. (11a)

Edison's original plan for his Fort Myers Estate was to share it with good friend and business partner Ezra Gilliland. Once the homes were built, Ezra bought the house and four acres on the south end of the property from Thomas. Soon after their relationship ended because of a business matter. After a number of owners, RIO Travers sold the property to Edison in 1906. For the next four years Edison remodeled the building to provide a Guest House for family and friends.

LEFT: The Dining Room in the Guest House became the only dining area on the Estate after the 1910 remodeling. The furnishings were custom made by Proctor and Company of New York City, based on an heirloom sideboard from Mina's family. Sadly, the original piece was lost during shipment to Fort Myers. (11b)

BELOW: Well-known guests who stayed in the Guest Home included (l to r) President Herbert Hoover, Henry Ford and Harvey Firestone seen posing with Edison near the riverbank. (11c)

EDISON'S SEMINOLE LODGE

LEFT: Southwest Bedroom. (12a)

BELOW: Both the Guest Wing and Family Wing of *Seminole Lodge* are seen in this image. A Pergola was added in 1910 that provided a walkway between the two homes, as well as provide a connection that created a sense of one estate. (12b)

ABOVE: Henry Ford's estate, *The Mangoes*, includes this view created by the palm alleé leading from the river to the back porch. (13a)

RIGHT: The Second Floor Study has one of the most spectacular views of the Caloosahatchee River. (13b)

ABOVE: *The Mangoes* is also decorated with casual wicker furniture to enhance comfort during winter retreats. The Living Room was used on occasion for one of Ford's favorite pastimes—square dancing. (13c)

Henry Ford first came to Fort Myers in 1914 at the invitation of Thomas Edison. In 1916 the owner of *The Mangoes*, Robert Smith of New York, asked Ford if he was interested in purchasing the property next to his good friend. After some negotiation, Ford agreed to buy the estate for $20,000. The visit of 1934 was the last time Henry stayed at this estate in Fort Myers. He rented the property for many years, and finally sold his estate in 1945 to local resident Thomas Biggar. *The Mangoes* was purchased in 1988 from the Biggar family.

LEFT: The Riverside Porch of *The Mangoes*. Such furnishings provided for additional space for warm winter evenings enjoyed outdoors. (14a)

BELOW: Edison relaxes with Clara and Henry Ford on the Front Porch of *The Mangoes*. (14b)

BOTTOM LEFT: The Ford Caretaker's Cottage, circa 1930. The Fords typically would only visit Fort Myers for several weeks during the year. This cottage enabled staff to stay on the property while looking after the grounds and home during the Fords' absence. (14c)

Ford auctioned off his original furnishings from *The Mangoes*. Today representative antiques and collectibles are placed in the home. The original Grandmother Clock is on display in the Estates Museum. The time on the clock is stopped at 11:40 p.m., an Irish tradition that tells the time of Ford's death on April 7, 1947.

Caloosahatchee River Walk

D

The Caloosahatchee River was, and remains, an important part of the Edison and Ford Winter Estates. The river provided the region with the primary transportation for most of its history. The train did not come to Fort Myers until 1904, and good roads for cars were created during the 1910s. Edison boated up the river from Punta Rassa to downtown Fort Myers on his first trip to the area in 1885. All of the original materials for his estate, from the clapboards to the linens, were brought by boat.

BELOW: Mina Edison found a breezy spot along the expanse of the seawall. The building of the seawall began in 1903 and was completed in 1907. As a dominant landscape feature of the estate, it created a family area with a beach, as well as to protect the pool and the property. (15a)

ABOVE: Thomas Edison and son Charles with their catch for the day. Fishing was a favorite hobby of the entire Edison family. In a 1906 letter Thomas notes "the finest Tarpon fishing in the world is right in front of my house in Florida." (15b)

BOTTOM RIGHT: A stunning contemporary view of the Edison Pier flowing out into the Caloosahatchee River. (15c)

BELOW: Guests gather at the summerhouse once located at the end of the Edison Pier, about 1917. The house was built in 1903 and was routinely used as a visiting area for family and friends. (15d)

CALOOSAHATCHEE RIVER WALK

15

During the 1920s, the popularity of aquatic flowers was growing. The Lily Pond landscape feature was added to the Edison grounds in 1929. The Pond provided an area for overflow water from the Pool, as well as a place for Mina to plant favorite botanicals such as iris, water lilies and papyrus.

ABOVE: A current view of the Lily Pond, which also has the grove of Coconut Palms adjacent to the feature. (16a)

BELOW: Thomas and Mina Edison pose at the Lily Pond. (16b)

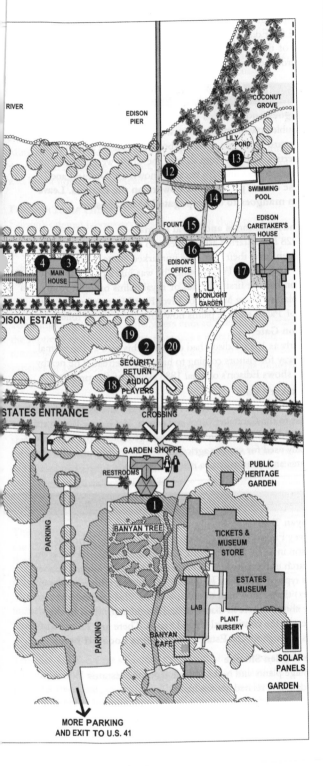

[Map labels:]

RIVER

EDISON PIER

COCONUT GROVE

LILY POND

13

12

SWIMMING POOL

14

EDISON CARETAKER'S HOUSE

FOUNT 15

4 3
MAIN HOUSE

16

EDISON'S OFFICE

17

MOONLIGHT GARDEN

EDISON ESTATE

19 2 20

SECURITY RETURN AUDIO PLAYERS

18

ESTATES ENTRANCE

CROSSING

GARDEN SHOPPE

RESTROOMS

1

BANYAN TREE

PARKING

PARKING

BANYAN CAFE

LAB

PUBLIC HERITAGE GARDEN

TICKETS & MUSEUM STORE

ESTATES MUSEUM

PLANT NURSERY

SOLAR PANELS

GARDEN

MORE PARKING AND EXIT TO U.S. 41

T: Madeleine (center) and others cool off
e Swimming Pool. The west side was
to the river where banana trees lined
wall and the view continued out to the
osahatchee River. (17a)

The Swimming Pool was first built in 1910
W.R. Wallace and Company, the same business
built the pool at the local Royal Palm Hotel.
1928, as part of the deal to move the original
to Michigan, Ford financed the remodeling of
pool complex. The new additions to the Pool
uded a Teahouse that provided an area to visit
icnic and a larger Bath House, all which were
nected to create one suite of buildings.

LEFT: The Swimming Pool was supplied
with water from the artesian well on the east
property. The pool is 50 feet long x 20 feet
wide and 4 to 7 feet deep. (17b)

BELOW: Friends strike a pose for the camera.
The original vertical board and batten fence
that once lined most of the Pool can be seen
in this image. (17c)

erfect
term
and
7d)

TOP LEFT: Contemporary view. (18a)

ABOVE: An early letter mentions the Fountain being used to cool off before the Pool was built, as can be seen here around 1907. (18b)

ABOVE: By 1928 large rocks surrounded the fountain feature and spout, covering up the smooth cement finish of earlier years. (18c)

RIGHT: Thomas gathers with a group of students from the Richmond Hill school. (18d)

The Rock Fountain was an early addition to improving the gardens. It was a significant feature of the Main Gate alleé that provided a stunning view from the entrance on through to the river. The Fountain became a favorite spot to gather.

LEFT: Henry Ford and Thomas Edison inspect the power system equipment located in the interior of the Lab upon its transfer to and placement at Greenfield Village. (19a)

MIDDLE LEFT: Henry and Clara Ford, along with Thomas and Mina Edison, pose for a photo in front of the Lab around 1928. (19b)

BOTTOM LEFT: Thomas Edison breaks from working in the Lab in 1912. (19c)

BELOW: Edison, Schumurica and Fred Ott contemplate a project. (19d)

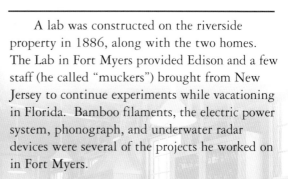

A lab was constructed on the riverside property in 1886, along with the two homes. The Lab in Fort Myers provided Edison and a few staff (he called "muckers") brought from New Jersey to continue experiments while vacationing in Florida. Bamboo filaments, the electric power system, phonograph, and underwater radar devices were several of the projects he worked on in Fort Myers.

By the mid-1920s Henry Ford began to collect historic buildings from around America and bring them to Dearborn, Michigan to a complex called Greenfield Village. All seven buildings from Edison's early Menlo Park, New Jersey complex were located at the site, as was the 1886 Fort Myers Lab. The Lab can be toured at Greenfield Village today, and was replaced with the Little Office and Moonlight Garden on the Fort Myers site.

This Little Office was built to replace a space Edison needed when the 1886 Lab was given to Ford's Greenfield Village. As part of the agreement, Ford paid for the construction of this building, so Edison could continue to have an office on the west grounds of the *Seminole Lodge*.

ABOVE: Edison stands near the front porch of the office, circa 1931. (20a)

TOP LEFT: Interior view of the office today. (20b)

MIDDLE LEFT: Original bottles labeled as chemicals used in research projects. (20c)

BELOW: Current view of the building. (20d)

Moonlight Garden

J

RIGHT: Mina and Carolyn examine plantings in the new garden. (21a)

BELOW: A recent restoration of the Moonlight Garden captures the essence of the original design and the way the Edison Family enjoyed the space. (21b)

LEFT: Mina and Thomas rest on bench. (21c)

The Moonlight Garden was created as an extension of the Little Office to provide a space for existing plantings, as well as for a garden. Ford also financed this feature. Reknowed female landscape architect Ellen Biddle Shipman, also a favorite of Clara Ford, initially designed the Garden. Together the two pieces follow the footprint of the 1886 Laboratory—giving a sense of where the lab once stood on the grounds.

ABOVE: The Caretaker's House recently underwent an extensive restoration. (22a)

RIGHT: June Scarth (Mates) poses by a tree in front of the House around 1930. Her father Sidney Scarth was the Edison driver for some 15 years. The original motor court and flower boxes are seen in this period image. (22b)

BOTTOM RIGHT: Tool house inventory of 1917. (22c)

EDISON CARETAKER'S HOUSE

Only part of the Caretaker's House existed on this section when Edison purchased the property from Samuel Summerlin in 1885. It was used as a stopover for cattle drovers moving herds down the road to Punta Rassa for shipment to Cuba. The Edisons expanded the building several times to accommodate staff typically brought down from New Jersey—as lab muckers, cooks and the driver. Some local help used the home, and it served as a caretaker's residence until 1991.

Tool House

    One combination gas engine
    One grubbing hoe
    One axe
    One crow bar
    One pair grass shears
    One pair pruning shears
    One mowing blade
    One hand saw
    One pick
    One potato fork
    One scythe and snath
    One weed digger
    One pitchfork
    One garden rake

LEFT: A view of McGregor Boulevard heading south, circa 1920. (23a)

RIGHT: Historic Riverside Avenue heading south, circa 1910. The cart traveling down the road represents a typical form of transportation of the time. (23b)

```
                                        SEMINOLE LODGE,
                                        Fort Myers, Fla.

To the Town Authorities of Ft. Myers,
     GENTLEMEN: If it is agreeable to the town, I will have royal
palms planted on both sides of the road from Manuel's Branch
creek to the end of Riverside avenue in the town, erect proper
protection crates, furnish fertilizer and humus for one year from
the time of planting, and make any necessary renewals of plants
for two years, providing the town will permit them to be located
at the most favorable position along the road, and a little out
of the ditch towards the road, and care for the trees and crates
after the expiration of the  periods mentioned. Should the town
accept, I will at once endeavor to procure the plants.

                              Yours Respectfully,
                                        Thomas A. Edison
```

ABOVE: Edison's letter to the Fort Myers "town authorities" asking them if they were agreeable to participating in planting and caring of Royal Palms down the street. (23c)

RIGHT: A postcard image of McGregor Boulevard driving northward. Also seen is the landmark Edison Park neighborhood entrance "Rachel by the Well" sculpture. (23d)

Riverside Avenue was the first main north to south road leading out from the City of Fort Myers to Punta Rassa. It was used extensively as a cattle trail. Edison originally envisioned Royal Poinciana Trees flanking both sides of Riverside Avenue along his property line. By 1907 Edison was ready to begin this endeavor, but changed his idea to using Royal Palm Trees. He decided to ask the City of Fort Myers to be a part of the plan. They agreed and the tradition continues for some ten miles. Fort Myers is known today as *The City of Palms.*

ABOVE: The Banyan, about 1936, is the tree on the right side of the photo, located on the east side of the original barn building. (24a)

LEFT: Edison examines a 12-foot-tall stock of goldenrod. (24b)

After several years of studying natural materials that produced latex, Edison began to plant hundreds of varieties on his Fort Myers property in 1924. The native India Banyan Tree on the property today was a gift of tire industrialist Harvey Firestone in 1925. At the time of planting the tree was 4 feet high and 2 inches in diameter. The majestic tree is now an acre in diameter and has some 350 roots.

BANYAN TREE

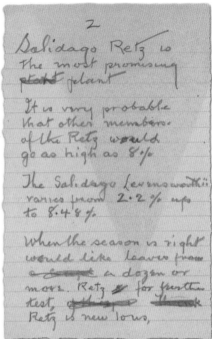

ABOVE: Guests experience the 1928 Lab today. (26a)

TOP RIGHT: A sample of research notes by Edison. Edison wrote out his ideas in a small notebook, and then a secretary would type them up and place the information in binders for future reference. (26b)

ABOVE: Exterior view of the Lab, circa 1930. (26c)

LEFT: (l to r) Henry Ford, Thomas Edison and Harvey Firestone await results of an experiment inside the Lab. (26d)

During World War I the price of rubber rose dramatically. Edison friends Henry Ford and Harvey Firestone were concerned with this issue. Thomas was troubled as well for many of his products contained elements made from rubber. His plan was to discover a domestic source of rubber from a latex (a white milky sap) producing plant. Florida's tropical climate was a perfect location for the project. The three friends formed the Edison Botanic Research Corporation in 1927 and the lab was built in 1928 to exclusively support the research and development. After Edison's death in 1931, the project continued a few more years and the Corporation was closed in 1936.

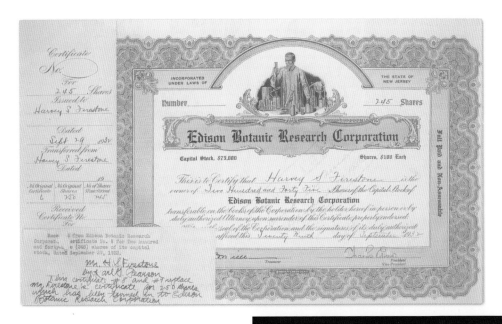

ABOVE: Original incorporation certificate for the EBRC project. (27a)

RIGHT: Original bottles. (27b)

BELOW: Interior view of the Lab today. All original materials and equipment, some containing rubber residue, remain from the project experiments. (27c)

RIGHT: One of the original typewriters still in the office. Azell Prince, Jr., Edison's secretary at the EBRC, remembered fondly typing notes up at this small desk area just behind "the old man's" desk. (28a)

LEFT: A group of unidentified staff poses at the back entrance to the newly constructed Laboratory. (28b)

BOTTOM LEFT: The actual Lab was last used during the summer of 1931. Hundreds of original apparatus and chemicals were left at the Lab, including the extraction units, of which this water condenser is a component. (28c)

BELOW: Each of Edison's labs include an office area for conducting business, writing up notes, storing office supplies, eating a snack, and taking a cat nap—at least for Mr. Edison. The EBRC office is set today as Azell Prince recalled. (28d)

LEFT: Interior view of the Lab, circa 1930. (29a)

MIDDLE LEFT: Experimental goldenrod sections and plots about 1934. Stakes labeled the variety of goldenrod planted. (29b)

BELOW: Edison walks along a field of goldenrod. (29c)

Edison's goal with the EBRC project was to produce a sufficient amount of rubber that could supply the nation during emergencies, especially during times of war. He set up a network of plant collectors and searched the United States, Puerto Pico, Cuba, and other countries for latex-producing plants. Some 17,000 specimens of nearly 2,200 species were planted at the Fort Myers estate. Edison's 1,090th patent received was connected to the rubber research, for the process of extracting rubber from plants.

The Estates Museum began in 1965 as the "Edison Science Museum," with artifacts relating to his many inventions and businesses. The Museum has grown through the years and includes gallery areas for exhibits, displays and additional educational and informative activities about Edison and Ford, their friends and families, Florida history, and other related topics.

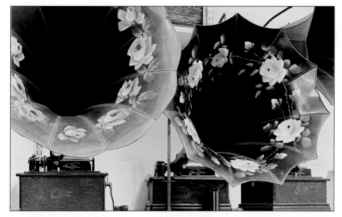

ABOVE: A 1940 V-8 Engine designed and developed by the Ford Motor Company. The artifact is on loan from The Henry Ford. (30a)

LEFT: Edison phonographs. (30b)

BELOW: Thomas Edison stands by his prized 1916 Model-T Ford Touring Car, a gift of Henry Ford. (30c)

RIGHT: Charles Edison (far left) unveils a bust of Edison to open the Museum in 1965 with the assistance of Director Robert Halgrim, Sr. and Mrs. Florence Black. (31a)

BELOW: Edison demonstrated his phonograph during a trip to Washington, D.C. to President Rutherford B. Hayes in 1879. This serving platter with a wild turkey design is from the White House china pattern of President Hayes. The Edison platter is from a set that would have been purchased in a department store. Not known is if Edison bought the piece, or if it was a gift. Whatever the circumstances, the platter without a doubt reminded Edison of his meeting with President Hayes. (31b)

LEFT: Commemorative light bulb by the General Electric Company. (31c)

BOTTOM LEFT: The 1916 Model-T Touring Car is a part of the Museum collection today. (31d)

BELOW: An Edison Stereophone—a movie would be seen with sound using the hearing device. (31e)

(32a)

"There is only one Fort Myers, and 90 million people are going to find it out."

THOMAS A. EDISON